That Strange Land

by

Sudie Thormahlen

DORRANCE
PUBLISHING CO
EST. 1920
PITTSBURGH, PENNSYLVANIA 15238

Dorrance Publishing Co
585 Alpha Drive
Suite 103
Pittsburgh, PA 15238
Visit our website at *www.dorrancebookstore.com*

Interior Design by Tracy Reedy

ISBN: 978-1-4809-5411-3
eISBN: 978-1-4809-5387-1

That Strange Land

I'll bet you ride a school bus or go to school in a car. Well, I have been to a strange land where the children can get to school by a sled with a team of dogs pulling them. It sounds strange, but I have been there and seen those dogs. It's the truth!!!

You have eaten salad before, I'm sure. Have you ever seen it made with a 50-pound cabbage? I have seen a cabbage that weighs as much as a young child . . . 50 pounds! That's one giant cabbage! It sounds strange, but I have been there and seen those cabbages. It's the truth!!!

Your bedtime is probably 8:00 or 9:00 P.M. What if you still had enough sunlight to play baseball or go fishing until almost midnight? There is a strange land like that.

Its nickname is Land of the Midnight Sun. It sounds strange, but I have been there and seen the sun that won't go to bed. It's the truth!!!

The wildlife in this strange land really is wild! We have seen black bear and maybe even a grizzly bear or two. This bear lives in very frigid areas and is the color of vanilla ice cream. It is called a polar bear and is usually even bigger than all other bears. It may sound strange, but I've been to that strange land. However, I did NOT see a polar bear but people who live there tell me it's the truth!

When we need to go someplace, we take a car, a pickup, or maybe a bus. If you live in big cities, you might take a taxi. In this strange land, people sometimes get on a plane just to play other sports teams because there is water surrounding the island they live on. This means the choices are boat, airplane or helicopter. Imagine wanting to play a rival football team and having to get on a plane to get there!! It may sound strange, but I have been there and that's what children have to do. It's the truth!

There are parts of this strange land that are so remote, far away from cities, that families have to have their food and supplies flown to them in a small plane every few weeks or even once a month. If they run out of meat, there are no groceries or big super stores. They might hunt a caribou, deer, or moose to have enough food to eat. If you run out of band aids or potato chips, you just have to substitute something else until the plane comes back. It may sound strange, but I have been there. It's the truth!

Many types of transportation are available in this strange land like plane, helicopter, dog sled, boat. What if you just wanted to go to a friend's house a short distance away though? Good news! Skis, snowshoes, and snowmobiles can keep you on top of the deepest snows. It sounds strange, but I have been there and seen it and it's the truth!

The lights almost vibrate and have a rhythm all their own. Like a child dancing, they bring your heart joy. They dance and whirl and twirl. It sounds strange, but I have been there and seen what is called the Aurora Borealis, or the Northern lights. They are beautiful and it's the truth!

We have all seen beautiful sunsets and sunrises. What if you saw a dancing rainbow in the sky? Blues and greens and reds, almost any color is a possibility. The colors don't stay still.

My favorite new bird I learned about while in this strange land is called a puffin. It looks like its creator had parts from lots of birds left over and put together this duck like bird. Their eyes are so dramatic, it looks like they have on fancy eye makeup. It lives on the hill-sides surrounding the ocean and dips and dives into the water for special treats. It sounds strange but I have been there and was delighted to find out it's the truth!

When the ice breaks up on the frozen rivers in this strange land, the salmon, a tasty, but truly ugly fish, rises to the top. When this happens, the bald eagles arrive by the thousands to take part in a fish feast. I saw 3 bald eagles in one tree. A local man told me he has seen as many as 10 in one tall bushy pine tree. It sounds strange, but I was there and it's the truth!

You have probably seen deer or elk, maybe even a moose or two. Have you ever seen reindeer? When raised on a farm, they are called reindeer, and when they are wild in the hills or plains or mountains, they are called caribou. It sounds strange, but I have been there and seen those strange looking creatures. It's the truth!!!

The people I have met there were warm and welcoming. Maybe they are so warm and kind because this strange land is so cold and people are far apart from each other. They seem genuinely happy to meet someone new and show you the wonders of their state. I was there and it's the truth!

I was lucky to see two types of whales and dolphins. The dolphins reminded me of kindergarten children, just released for recess-dashing about, jumping and throwing their heads back with a strange high-pitched giggle sound. It felt like they were all best friends and enjoyed being together so much. It sounds strange, but I was there and saw them and it's the truth!

Another rare treasure in this strange land is gold. That's right…real genuine gold. They found it hundreds of years ago in the creeks, rivers and glaciers of ice. They still mine and pan for it today. Tourists like to buy jewelry made from gold. Rings, necklaces, earrings and watches are all available. It might sound strange, but I was there and saw it and it's the truth!

I would guess that by now you are saying, "Where is this strange land and what is it called? Is it in outer space or in the ocean?" No, it is in the United States of America. It is called Alaska. I went there and saw many strange things. It's the truth. You should go there and tell me what strange new things you discover. I will believe you and know it's the truth!!!

CPSIA information can be obtained
at www.ICGtesting.com
Printed in the USA
LVHW071158090419
613499LV00009B/165/P